We Scream for Ice Cream

Bernice Chardiet and Grace Maccarone
pictures by G. Brian Karas

SCHOLASTIC INC.

New York   Toronto   London   Auckland   Sydney

P9-CEF-351

To Molly and Mia
B.C.

To Matt, Larry, Alan, and Dennis
G.M.

To Sara
G.B.K.

ISBN 0-590-44934-6

Copyright © 1992 by Grace Maccarone and Chardiet Unlimited, Inc.

12 11 10 9 8 7 6 5 4 3 2 1   2 3 4 5 6 7/9

Printed in the U.S.A.   08

First Scholastic printing, April 1992

Ting-a-ling-ding-dong.
Ting-a-ling-ding-dong.
The Rooty-Tooty ice cream truck
was coming down the street.

Bunny and Cynthia were doing their
homework together at Cynthia's house.
"Ma! Can we get ice cream?" Cynthia asked.
"Here's some money," said her mother.
"There's enough for both of you."

Outside, the girls saw their school friends,
Martin and Sammy, going to the Rooty-Tooty truck.
Raymond Allen Tally was first on line.
His initials spelled R.A.T.,
and that's what all the kids called him.
R.A.T. had his dog, Animal, with him.

Bunny and Cynthia joined the line.
Then Brenda came along
with her little brother, Truman.
She pushed in front of Cynthia.
"Can't you see that this is a line?"
Cynthia said. "I was here first."
Brenda and Truman had to go to the back.

"What are you getting?" Bunny asked.
"I'm getting a double chocolate ice cream bar,"
said Brenda. "If you get an ice cream stick
with a picture of Rooty-Tooty on it,
it's a Lucky Stick. You win a free
ice cream sundae."

"I'm getting a strawberry cone," said Sammy.
"Don't get a cone," said Martin. "You can't
get a Lucky Stick with a cone."
"I don't care," said Sammy. "I want
a strawberry cone."

"Hey! Tell your ugly dog to stop sniffing my baby brother," Brenda said to R.A.T. "I'm not a baby!" said Truman. "Who are you calling ugly?" R.A.T. said.

The Rooty-Tooty lady called out,
"May I help someone? Who's first?"
"I am," R.A.T. said. "I'll have a root beer float."

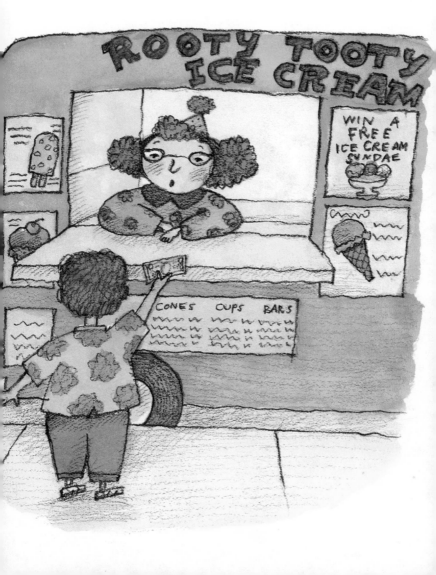

Martin got a Chocolate Nutty bar,
and Sammy got his strawberry cone.

Bunny asked for a Rooty-Tooty-Frooty bar.
She had never tasted one before,
but she liked the name.

"What can I get for you today?"
the Rooty-Tooty lady asked Cynthia.
"I'll have a vanilla bar,"
Cynthia said. "No, that's boring.
I'll have a Frooty Coconut bar.
No. I might not like the coconut.
I'll have a Berry-Tooty-Nutty bar.
But berries make me itchy..."

"Hurry up," said Brenda.
"You're taking too much time.
Make up your mind."
"Oh, I'll have a rainbow ice,"
Cynthia said quickly.

After one lick, Cynthia knew
she had made a mistake.
She didn't like her rainbow ice at all.
Bunny didn't like her Rooty-Tooty-Frooty
bar either.

Brenda was next. "I'll have
a double chocolate bar for myself
and a vanilla cup for my brother,"
said Brenda.

"I want ice cream on a stick,"
said Truman.
"No," said Brenda. "You'll
just spill it and make a mess.
Here. Take your cup."

"I don't want a cup," Truman shouted.
"I want ice cream on a stick!
I want ice cream on a stick!"
Truman threw his ice cream on the ground.

Cynthia picked up the cup and spoon.
She threw them in the litter basket.
"You shouldn't litter," Cynthia said.

Truman started to cry.
"I don't have any ice cream," he sobbed.
"You can have mine," said Bunny.

Truman sniffled.
"Thank you," he said.

Truman tried to make his
Rooty-Tooty-Frooty bar
last as long as possible.
But it was melting quickly.
"You have to eat faster," Brenda said.

"Okay," said Truman
and he took a big bite.
The Rooty-Tooty-Frooty ice cream
dropped onto the sidewalk.

"You made me do that!" Truman yelled.
He threw the ice-cream stick at Brenda.
"I did not. You're just clumsy!"
Brenda yelled back.

Truman grabbed Brenda's arm,
and her ice cream fell, too.

Brenda looked down. She saw something
on Truman's ice cream stick.
It was a picture of Rooty-Tooty!
Truman had a Lucky Stick!

Brenda bent down and pretended
to tie her shoelace.
Quickly she grabbed the Lucky Stick.

Bunny saw her do it.
"It's mine!" said Bunny.
"I bought it."

"No, it's mine," said Cynthia.
"You used my mother's money."

"It's mine," said Truman.
"Bunny gave it to me!"

"Finders keepers, losers weepers,"
said Brenda. She waved the stick
in the air. "Now it's MINE!"

R.A.T. was watching. "Fetch!" he said to Animal.
Animal jumped up and grabbed the Lucky Stick.
"Ha! Ha! My dog has the Lucky Stick,
so it's mine," said R.A.T.

"Good dog," R.A.T. said to Animal.
"Give me the stick!"
But Animal ran away.
R.A.T. ran after Animal and bumped into Martir
The root beer float flew out of R.A.T.'s hand.
It plopped to the ground.

"Let's get out of here," Sammy said to Martin.
"This is a dangerous place to eat ice cream."

Now, only Cynthia's rainbow ice
was left, but not for long.
"I hate rainbow ice," said Cynthia.
She let it drip and drip until
it was just a puddle on the sidewalk.

"What a mess," said Bunny.

"What a waste," said Brenda.

"We'd better clean it up," said Cynthia.

"Someone could slip in it and get hurt."

Truman and the girls cleaned up the mess.

"Look! R.A.T.'s coming back," Truman said.
"Do you have the Lucky Stick?" he asked.
"No," said R.A.T.

Truman cried louder than ever.
Everyone felt terrible.

"I'm sorry," said Brenda.
"I shouldn't have been so greedy."
"I'm sorry, too," said Bunny.
"The Lucky Stick was really Truman's.
I gave it to him."

"Well, I still think I should have
gotten something," Cynthia said.
"No one would have had the stick
if I hadn't lent Bunny the money."
"So what?" said R.A.T. "All that means
is that Bunny owes you a dollar."

"I know what!" said Bunny. "I have some
Fruity Chewies at home. We can share them."

"I'll go home and get some cookies,"
said Cynthia. "My dad and I baked them."

"Then we can go to my house," said Brenda.
"I'll share my swings."

Everybody had fun.
It was a good day after all.

And tomorrow, the ice cream truck
would come again, *ting-a-ling-ding-dong*
down the street.